For Jaxon, our star

First published in 2019 by Child's Play (International) Ltd
Ashworth Road, Bridgemead, Swindon SN5 7YD, UK

Published in USA in 2020 by Child's Play Inc
250 Minot Avenue, Auburn, Maine 04210

Distributed in Australia by Child's Play Australia Pty Ltd
Unit 10/20 Narabang Way, Belrose, Sydney, NSW 2085

Text copyright © 2019 Jana Novotny Hunter
Illustrations copyright © 2019 Child's Play (International) Ltd
The moral rights of the author and illustrator have been asserted

ISBN 978-1-78628-298-9
CLP020719CPL08192989

Printed and bound in Shenzhen, China

1 3 5 7 9 10 8 6 4 2

A catalogue record of this book
is available from the British Library

www.childs-play.com

CIRCUS
★ GIRL ★

Jana Novotny Hunter

illustrated by

Joaquín Camp

Sky dreams...

She dreams of clowns,
She dreams of acrobats,
She dreams of stardust;
All the fun of the circus!

And Sky is the ringmaster!

Sky!

She dreams of red,
She dreams of blue,
She dreams of gold;
All the colors
of the circus!

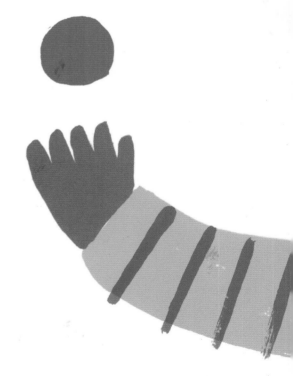

And Sky is the juggler!

She dreams of peanuts,
She dreams of popcorn,
She dreams of pretzels;
All the smells of the circus!

And Sky is the tightrope walker!

There's laughter, cheering and music
as Sky dreams...

Until, awake at last,
she starts to get ready for school.

And as she puts
on her shirt...

Sky hears the crowd clap!

And as she grabs her books...

Sky hears
the crowd roar!

BREAKFAST
IS READY!

Sky dreams
of the circus
so much...

that she's sometimes
late for breakfast.

Late for breakfast, but not for school!

Sky is never late for school,
because Sky loves to learn.

At school...

At home...

And especially...

...under
the big top!

After school,
Sky gets busy...

Carting, carrying, and lifting,
Holding, shouldering, and shifting.

Then Sky practices her circus skills;
Spinning, twisting, and turning,
Swivelling, twirling, and whirling!

Because on the weekends,
Sky and her troupe perform.

Hanging, leaping, and landing,
Dangling, swinging, and standing
on the balance bar.

Hurrah!

And that's when...